PAUL KROPP

EMC Publishing, St. Paul, Minnesota

Library of Congress Cataloging in Publication Data

Kropp, Paul.
  Baby, baby.
  (Encounters series/Paul Kropp)
  Summary: Dave convinces Lori that when two
people love each other anything they do is all
right. When Lori gets pregnant, however, they
find out that love is not enough.
  [1. Pregnancy—Fiction. 2. Unmarried
mothers—Fiction. 3. Unmarried fathers—
Fiction] I. Gulland, Sandra. II. Collins,
Heather, ill. III.Title. IV. Series: Kropp,
Paul. Encounters series.
PZ7.K93Bab 1983   [Fic]   82-12931
ISBN 0-88436-962-5

Published by EMC Publishing
300 York Avenue
Saint Paul, Minnesota 55101

Printed in the United States of America
0 9 8 7 6 5 4 3 2

CONTENTS

CHAPTER

Baby, baby, don't say no to me.
Baby, baby, I won't let you be.
Don't say no 'cause it's you and me,
So in love that you'll never be free.

Lori always felt all misty when Dave sang
this song—her song. Even now, packed
into the school gym with two hundred
other kids, she was moved by the words.
The other kids weren't listening to the
words. They were talking or dancing close
or just goofing around. They didn't know
that Dave had written this one song just
for her.

She watched Dave up on stage. The sweat poured off him as he sang, and it made his face gleam under the colored lights. Anyone could see that Dave was good-looking. He seemed to have stepped right off an album cover. What the others couldn't see was the person inside who was so gentle and caring. When Dave sang "Baby, Baby" it was the person inside that Lori saw.

The band finished the number and got a little applause from the kids on the dance floor. Lori came out of her trance and looked around, wondering where her friend Janet had gone. There was nothing she hated more than being left alone at a dance. Now that Janet had wandered off, Lori was by herself.

The band switched to an old Buddy Holly number in which Dave played backup guitar. Lori knew just which number came next because she had been hanging around the band for a month, helping to pick songs for each set. It was a good time to look for Janet.

Before she got very far, a girl from her history class grabbed her arm. "Lori, the band is great and Dave is a hunk!"

Another girl said, "I bet half the stuff
he sings is just for you, eh?"

Lori smiled. "Have you seen Jan in
the past couple minutes?" At school all
the kids shortened Janet to Jan.

One girl pointed to the girl's
washroom down the hall, so Lori shouted
her thanks and headed off that way.

"I wondered what happened to you,"
Lori said when she found Janet. Her
friend was fixing her make-up in front of
the washroom mirror.

"I got tired of waiting for Dennis to
ask me to dance," Janet told her,

tightening her lips to put on some lipstick. "You'll never guess what all the kids are saying. Everybody thinks that Dave is a great-looking guy. Maggie said that Dave was so good he should take over lead guitar."

Lori had always thought that Dave was handsome, with big shoulders and eyes that seemed to look right through a girl. But it still made her feel good to hear that her friends felt the same way.

"What are they saying about the band?" Lori asked.

"Well, the kids seem to like it, I guess.

They say it's pretty good for a high-school band, except for the name. Maggie thinks that Western Lights is kind of strange," Janet said.

"Does she have any better ideas?" Lori asked, a little angry since she had helped pick the name.

"Yeah, she thought you should call them the Little Rubber Band, so I told her I'd bounce the idea off you," Janet answered.

"Tell her to go shoot her rubber bands someplace else. The Western Lights are doing just fine," Lori said. "They're going to play at a club right after Thanksgiving."

"Hey, that's great," Janet said.

The two of them pushed out of the washroom and fought their way through the crowd of girls in the hall outside.

"Are you going to wait around here while they pack up or do you want to walk home with me?" Janet asked.

"What do you think?" Lori asked, laughing at the choice.

"Stupid question. Look, I'm going to bug Mr. O'Donnell to dance the next slow one with me, so I'll see you later."

"For sure," Lori said as she went back inside the gym.

"And if I don't see you later," her friend added, turning back for a second, "don't do anything I wouldn't do."

After the dance Lori had to wait for over an hour while the band packed all its stuff into the van. It would be nice, she thought, if the Western Lights had roadies to do all the cleaning up. But the band was just getting started, and any kind of real road show would be years away.

"That's it," Dave said, wrapping his arm around Lori. "So you think the show looked pretty good?"

"I told you already," Lori answered. "Even Maggie said you were super, and she never says anything good about anybody."

"Did you hear me sing 'Baby, Baby' for you?" he asked.

"I felt all misty, just like always," Lori told him.

"I was thinking about you tonight when I was up there on stage," Dave went on. "You're very special to me."

"Dave," she said, whispering his name. Lori felt a little awkward standing with him in the corner of the gym. The other guys in the band were still hanging around.

"I got a present for you because ..." Dave began, trying to think of the right words. "Well, just because."

He reached into his coat pocket and pulled out a tiny box. Lori took it from his hand and couldn't help but smile. There was something about this gesture that was so much like Dave—a little shy, a little awkward and yet so thoughtful.

Lori opened the box to find a gold chain with a white heart on it. She lifted the necklace out of the box and held it in her hand.

"Oh, Dave, it's beautiful," she said, her voice choked with tears.

"Let me put it on you," he offered.

Lori couldn't even speak to tell him yes. Dave took the golden chain, opened the clasp and put it gently around Lori's neck.

"You do like it, don't you?" he asked, unsure of himself.

"I love it," she said. Then Lori kissed

11

him, in spite of the brightly lit gym, in spite of the other band members still around them.

"Better cool it," the lead guitar player broke in. "Keep that up and you never know what kind of trouble you'll end up in."

Dave just grinned in reply. He took Lori's hand and led her to the van parked outside.

CHAPTER

"Hey, Lori, where are you?" Janet asked over the phone.

"Look, flea-brain, if you call my house and I answer, that gives you a pretty good idea where I am."

"O.K., so I'm stupid. But you said you were going to help me babysit, remember? Besides, I need help with those questions for history."

"Sorry, Jan, I forgot," Lori told her. "I'll be right over."

Lori hadn't been thinking about Janet at all. She was still upset over a fight she'd had with her mother. Lori got tired of hearing the same old things—"Why were you out so late?" "Why don't you go out with other boys?"

Lori knew that her mother kept throwing questions at her because she cared about her, but that didn't make it any easier. Lori had tried to tell her mother about Dave, but it didn't help. Her mother still thought that sixteen was too young to be seeing just one boy.

The air outside was cold and the wind blew Lori's dark hair back from her face. It was only two blocks to Janet's house, but she felt chilled by the time she got there.

Lori could hear the baby crying even before she got inside the house. "Sounds like I got here just in time," she said as she took off her coat.

"The baby's just awful, Lori. He's got gas or something and just will not settle down."

Lori picked up the baby and rocked him in her arms. Then she put him against her shoulder and patted his back. Lori rocked the baby as if there were nothing easier in the world for her, and at last he fell asleep.

"You sure have a way with kids," Janet whispered. The baby was asleep and she didn't want to start him crying again. She watched as Lori carefully laid the baby in the crib.

"Where's Tammy?" Lori asked as they sat down at the table in the kitchen.

"On a date," Janet explained.

"So you end up babysitting again? Are you getting the usual pay?"

"Yeah, a handshake and a smile is about all that Tammy can afford," Janet said. "Tammy's having a hard enough time, so I help out when I can."

"It must be rough trying to be both mother and father," Lori said.

"Yeah, it's not easy for her," Janet agreed. "What were you so angry about when I called you? You have another fight with your mother?"

"How'd you guess?"

"The first clue I had was when you called me 'flea-brain' on the telephone. But I figured that you two would have a fight when you came back late from the dance."

"I wasn't even that late," Lori said, shaking her head. "I tried to tell her that it takes over an hour to tear down but she doesn't understand. She thinks we were making out in the van. Sometimes it seems all parents ever think about is sex."

"Yeah, parents and boyfriends," Janet said with a sigh. "When I was going out with Mike all he could think about was getting in the back seat and ... you know."

"You never—"

"Of course I didn't," Janet snapped, blushing. "You think I'd play around after what happened to Tammy? I mean, I might be a flea-brain, but I'm not a no-brain."

Lori thought how much easier it must have been for Janet to say no, since Janet had never been in love with Mike.

The two girls had just begun work on Janet's history homework when Janet's sister came in the front door.

"Tammy!" Janet said with some surprise.

"Hi, Lori. How's my little Ian?" Tammy asked before walking softly toward the bedroom. She peeked in quickly at the sleeping baby and then came back to the kitchen.

"He's not crying," Tammy said. "It must be the first time in days. I think he's teething or something."

"You're back sort of early," Janet said, looking up at the wall clock.

"The guy was the pits," Tammy told her. "His idea of a date was, 'I'll buy you dinner and then we'll go back to my place.' So when he came on, I told him to buzz off."

"Whatever happened to all the decent guys?" Janet asked.

"I've got one," Lori said proudly.

"Don't count too much on that," Tammy warned. "Even the nicest guy in the world can get in over his head, especially when he's in love. The thing is, you can't expect even a decent guy to set the bottom line for you—you've got to do that for yourself."

"Sounds like women's lib," Lori said.

"Maybe it is," Tammy went on. "All I know is that you'd better start looking out for yourself because nobody else is going to."

"Don't you think that's a little strong?" Lori asked.

"The whole thing with John and the baby didn't leave me with a lot of faith in other people," Tammy admitted. "But now that I'm back in Denver with mom and dad and Jan, things have worked out all right. Still, I've lost an awful lot of time out of my life. What do you think it's like when you're older than anyone else in class?"

"It must be pretty strange," Lori said. She knew that Tammy had dropped out of school even before she got pregnant. Now she was going to eleventh grade classes over at Central.

"Well, 'strange' might be a nice word for it. Sometimes these sixteen-year-olds in class drive me so nuts I think I might quit. But I can't do that again. I'm going to finish high school and get a decent job, only this time I'm not going to get sidetracked."

"By men?" Janet asked.

"By anything. I know when I was your age I was pretty stupid. I didn't know what I wanted out of life, so I let other people make decisions for me. I got pregnant because I didn't think enough to be careful. There must be half a dozen different kinds of birth control, and I was so stupid I didn't use any of them."

"In health class the teacher said that 80 per cent of kids our age don't use anything the first time," Janet said.

"A lot of girls expect the guy to take care of it," Tammy explained. "But most of the time they don't bother, so it's really up to the girl to control things."

"If I was on the pill and my mother found out, she'd kill me," Lori told them.

"You might be surprised what your mom would say if you asked her, Lori. Birth control makes a lot more sense than

22

getting pregnant."

"I suppose," Lori said.

The baby started crying in the bedroom and Tammy got up to go to him. But she stopped and turned toward Lori before she left the room.

"Let me give you some free advice," Tammy offered. "The best way not to get pregnant isn't anything you get from a doctor or a drugstore. It's a two-letter word — no."

CHAPTER

Two weeks later.
When the Western Lights opened at the Lollyberry, they didn't pack the house. Lori was there, of course, and Janet went with her. A few people came along who knew other members of the band, but otherwise the place was empty. Lori knew that there wouldn't be many people out on a Tuesday, but it still bothered her. She thought that the band deserved to play to a real crowd.

And she was right. The band had worked for weeks trying to turn their music into a real show. They had matched the lights with the numbers in each set and learned to move together on stage. All their work had paid off in some really good sets.

"I just think there should be more people here," Lori sighed.

"Your mother offered to come," Janet reminded her.

"She only wanted to make sure I got home on time. Besides, that's not what I meant," Lori explained.

"What can you expect?" Janet asked. "It's Tuesday night, it's freezing outside and no one's ever heard of the Western Lights. Maybe they could have fooled more people into coming if they were called the Little Rubber Band."

"Oh, cut it out."

"Well, look, it was just an idea," Janet said, sipping her Coke.

Lori wasn't mad at Janet. She was just angry that the crowd was so small when the band was playing so well.

"How come they're playing so much country-and-Western?" Janet asked.

"They want to branch out a little so they can get more gigs," Lori told her.

"That's too bad," Janet said. "I like

their rock numbers a lot better, and that song 'Baby, Baby.'"

"Me, too," Lori sighed.

When the last set was over, Dave flopped into a chair next to Lori. He was tired and thirsty from singing and he seemed a little down.

Lori curled her fingers into his hair as she leaned against him. "You were super," she told him softly.

"Yeah, but there was hardly anybody to hear it," Dave said. "Even Jan left before the end of the last set."

"Her dad was waiting to pick her up," Lori explained. "You know Jan really likes the music. Just wait until next week after word gets around about how wonderful you are."

"Hey," he said, looking into her eyes, "you're good for me, you know that? When everything else has got me down I can just look at you and I feel O.K. again." Dave took Lori's hand in his.

"Why don't we get out of here," Dave suggested. "We don't have to tear down, so I'll just grab my guitar and we can head off in the van."

The two of them got their heavy coats
and left the Lollyberry. When they
reached the van in the parking lot, Dave
unlocked the door for Lori first. Then he
climbed into the driver's side as she slid
across the front seat to be next to him.

"Are you in a hurry to get home?"
Dave asked. He turned the key and the
old van came alive.

"Not really," she said. "I already had a
fight with my mother about coming down
here, so what difference does it make
when I get home?"

"Well, it must make some difference,"

Dave told her. "You don't want to be out too late or you'll be grounded for life. Let's go over to that spot on 149th Ave. and talk for a while before I take you home, O.K.?"

Lori answered him with a kiss.

It was a long drive to the parking spot on 149th Ave., but Lori didn't mind. She kept thinking back about Dave singing to her from up on stage. There was something about him when he was up on stage, something special that made her feel important. The music for "Baby, Baby" was running through her mind when Dave pulled the van into a parking spot.

"So were we really good?" Dave asked as he turned off the motor.

"You were only, uh, well, wonderful," Lori said. She was teasing him with her words and her hands.

"You really mean it?" Dave asked, smiling at the way she touched him.

"I really mean it," she answered, lifting her head to kiss him lightly on the lips. "I just felt so . . . I don't even know how to say it, when you were singing up there."

"Hey, that's really nice." Dave kissed her softly on the cheek, then again on her chin. "Maybe you should have brought your mother after all," he said, grinning.

"She doesn't like rock music at all. The only reason she wanted to come along was to check up on me," Lori told him.

"She doesn't like me, does she?" Dave asked.

"It's not you—she wouldn't like anybody I went out with. Ever since dad left her I think she's had this thing about men."

"Maybe you just don't give her a chance," Dave said.

"Maybe she should have a little more trust in me, huh? She's afraid that I'm going to fall in love and drop out of high school."

"Would you do that?" Dave asked.

"I can't see why I'd have to give up going to school," Lori said.

"That's not what I meant," Dave whispered. "Would you fall in love?"

With one hand Dave gently touched Lori's cheek as he searched for an answer in her eyes.

"I already have," Lori whispered to him.

"Oh, Lori, Lori . . ." Dave began, then lost her name as he kissed her.

Lori felt his arms holding her, pulling her tightly against him. She loved the strong manly smell of him after he sang, the power in his arms and hands as he reached for her.

"I love you, Lori," he said over and over, kissing her eyes, nose, and lips. Lori responded to him look for look, kiss for kiss, touch for touch.

"I think we'd be a little more comfortable in the back of the van," Dave whispered.

"I think we'd be more comfortable right here," Lori said, drawing away from him.

"Come on, Lori," Dave said, looking right at her. "You said you loved me."

"I do, but . . . I don't want to," Lori answered, fighting back the urge to say yes. She wanted to keep everything under control. But Dave's kisses and his words were making it harder to say no.

"Nothing is going to happen that you don't want to happen," Dave told her. He kissed her lightly on the cheeks.

Still Lori sat without saying anything. She was so full of wanting that she could barely control her own voice.

"When two people love each other, anything they do works out," Dave went on, taking her hands.

"Dave," she said, whispering his name.

He kissed her once more, and then she followed him to the back of the van.

CHAPTER

When Dave brought Lori home, it was so late that she had to sneak into the house. In the living room her mother had fallen asleep in front of the TV set. For just a moment Lori thought she should stop to wake her, but she felt guilty enough without that. She didn't want to face her mother, not now.

Lori didn't know why she felt so down. Love was supposed to be filled with joy and sharing. Lori only felt tired and upset over what had happened. It was a lot less wonderful than she had expected.

Lori felt better in the morning—less guilty and even a little proud.

"You must have been pretty late," her mother said over breakfast.

"I thought you were in bed when I came in, but it wasn't much past midnight," Lori lied. She felt bad about lying and covering up.

"Well, I fell asleep in front of the TV waiting for you," her mother told her. She gave Lori a look that seemed to see right through her lie.

"I didn't go into the living room," Lori explained.

"How did the opening night go?"

"They played really well," Lori answered, "but the place was almost empty."

"I should have gone with you and added to the crowd," her mother said.

"You wouldn't have liked it," Lori told her. The more they talked about the night before, the more embarrassed she became.

"Did you and Dave go out afterward?" her mother asked.

Lori was certain that her face was turning red. She covered her cheeks with her hands and looked down at her coffee without speaking.

"I thought they might have had a party afterward. When I was in high school we always had parties after the first night of a play."

"It's different for a rock band, mom," Lori said.

"I guess things are very different from when I was in school and we all lived in caves." Lori's mother smiled, but Lori didn't look up to see it.

"Yeah."

"Look, Lori, I don't want to stick my

nose in where it doesn't belong, but it seems to me that you're spending an awful lot of time with Dave."

"I guess that's true," Lori answered, looking out the window. She knew she was going to get either a lecture or a bunch of embarrassing questions.

"What I mean is—you are careful, aren't you?"

"What is that supposed to mean?" Lori said, embarrassed by the question. She hadn't been careful the night before. It wasn't as if she had planned things to happen the way they did.

"You know perfectly well what I mean," her mother said. "A lot of men are just like your father. They seem to be people you can count on, but—"

"Stop bad-mouthing my father," Lori snapped.

"And you can stop raising your voice when you talk to me, Lori."

"Well, I don't need all these questions," Lori almost shouted at her mother. "I know you don't like Dave, but that's no reason to ... to suggest things all the time."

"Dave is just like all the other boys,"

her mother lectured.

"No, he's not! He's special to me, and if you understood that ... well, then you wouldn't talk the way you do." Lori was crying now, not so much because of her mother but because of her own worry and guilt. She pushed back her chair and stood up, spilling the rest of her coffee on the table.

"Lori, I'm trying to understand ...."

But Lori didn't wait for her mother to finish. She threw on her coat and ran outside, where the tears on her cheeks felt cold in the winter air.

Lori didn't hear what was going on in her classes that morning—her thoughts were on other things. Dave said he loved her and she thought she loved him. Other people could say what they wanted to, but Dave and Lori were in love and love was enough.

But love wasn't enough to stop Lori's fears. What if she were pregnant? She told herself that the chances were small, but why had she taken any chance at all? Tammy had said that the best way not to get pregnant was to say no. Why couldn't Lori have kept saying no?

Maybe all Dave's talk of love was nothing more than talk. There was always the chance that he'd be finished with her now. That's what had happened to Maggie after she went all the way with Frank Albers. He dumped her so fast that Maggie didn't even know what was happening.

Of course, Dave wasn't like that. Lori knew that he was someone she could trust, someone who really cared for her. Still, Lori wondered how many other girls there had been before her. In health class they had talked about VD, and there was always a chance . . . .

"Lori, you're white as a sheet!"

Lori stood back from her locker and saw Janet looking right at her.

"Did you have a fight with your mother?" Janet asked.

"Yeah, sort of," Lori told her, not ready yet to come out with what was really bothering her.

"What happened — you get back too late from the Lollyberry?"

"Yeah, *real* late."

"Oh," Janet said, reading something strange in Lori's words, a secret that lay behind them. Both of the girls stood there while other students grabbed lunches from their lockers and rushed off to eat.

"O.K., what's really the matter?" Janet asked. There was a long silence while she waited for an answer.

"You know," Lori began, looking away from her friend. "Dave and I, we . . . ." She was too upset to say what they had done, but still wanted to share it with her friend.

"Oh, I see." Janet cleared her throat and smiled to see Lori looking so red in the face. She looked up and down the hall

to make sure no one was around before she added, "You don't look very happy about it."

"Well, I'm a little worried," Lori said, closing her locker.

"You're not—you know—in trouble, are you?" Janet asked in a whisper.

"No, nothing like that," Lori told her, though she wasn't quite as sure as she sounded. "At least, not yet."

CHAPTER

One month later.
"I don't like doing this, you know," Janet
said as Lori took off her coat.

"Don't be such a goody-goody," Lori
told her. "You're not doing anything at
all—I'm the one who could end up
grounded for life."

Lori was right in a way. All she had
asked was that Janet cover for her in
case Lori's mother should check up on
her. Chances were good that Lori's
mother wouldn't call at all.

"Why don't you just tell your mother
that you're going out with Dave?"

"She already thinks I'm seeing too much of him, so she laid down this new rule," Lori explained. "Fridays and Saturdays only. When the band gets a job, that means I don't see him at all. That's pretty rotten, don't you think?"

"Seems like plenty to me," Janet said as she watched Lori put on her make-up. "You shouldn't use so much eye shadow — it makes you look cheap."

"I think it makes me look sexy," Lori said, blinking at herself in the mirror. "And I don't think twice a week is enough. Besides, Dave's parents are out, so we have the house to ourselves." Lori stopped talking so she could put on some lipstick. She couldn't put on make-up at home because that would be a dead giveaway.

Janet didn't like the changes she had seen in Lori in the past month. After the first night with Dave, Lori had been scared and upset. But a few days later she had forgotten her fears. Lori hadn't gotten pregnant that first time because her luck had been good. Now she was seeing Dave more, and it was only a matter of time until her luck ran out.

"I still don't like it," Janet complained. "You really think she'll believe me if I tell her you went down to the store?"

"Jan, my mother would believe anything *you* told her. Tell her I was kidnapped by the ghost of George Washington. It's not what you say, it's the way you say it, and you look like you've never told anyone a lie in your entire life."

"Thanks a lot," Janet said, staring at herself in the mirror. Lori was right, of course. Janet's blonde hair and baby face made her look like a perfect angel, and she hated that.

Off in the bedroom little Ian began to cry. Janet went to the kitchen to warm up a bottle for him. This was the second time that Ian had been up since Tammy went out.

"I'll get him," Lori called as she went back to the bedroom. She came out rocking the baby in her arms, but it didn't do any good. "I guess he's hungry," she said.

"Yeah, either he's hungry or he needs a change or he's sick. Sometimes it really gets me down," Janet sighed.

"Well, look," Lori began, "I didn't want to get into this, but don't you think Tammy is asking a bit much? I mean, your mother babysits Ian all day when she's at school, and then you end up babysitting at night. When does Tammy take care of her own child?"

"When she can," Janet answered, a little angry at Lori's words.

"Look, don't get upset," Lori told Janet as she handed the baby to her. "I'm your friend, so it's my job to tell you what I think."

"Is that what friends are supposed to

48

do?" Janet snapped. "Well, maybe I should tell *you* a few things, because I've been keeping my mouth shut for weeks."

"Not now, Jan—Dave will be driving up any minute."

"Then maybe this is the right time, Lori. You're changing—you know that? You never used to sneak around behind your mother's back like this. All you ever think of now is Dave, Dave, Dave, and I wonder if he's really worth it. It wasn't bad until, well, you know. But now it's like he's taken over your whole life and you can't even think about anything else."

"We're in love," Lori said simply.

"Well, that's wonderful, but you'd better start watching out for yourself. I think everybody in school knows that you and Dave are fooling around."

"Nobody cares about it except you," Lori told her.

"How can you be so sure?" Janet asked. The baby was still crying, but she went ahead. "You know who came up to me at school and asked about you? Maggie! She wanted to know if you were pregnant yet or what. And if Maggie knows, you can bet that she told Liz and

Dennis and everybody else in school."

"So who cares what people think they know," Lori said, getting angry herself. "I don't care about a bunch of jealous fleabrains who don't know anything but keep on shooting their mouths off. What did you say to her, anyway?"

"What could I say?" Janet asked.

"You could tell her to shut up and mind her own business," Lori almost shouted.

"And what good is that going to do?" Janet said in a lower voice. She got Ian's bottle of milk from the kitchen, and that kept him quiet. "Look, I don't want to fight with you about this and I know you think you're in love with Dave. Maybe I know better than anyone just what you're going through right now. But you've got to be more careful—just ask my sister."

"I'm not going to get pregnant, believe me," Lori told her. "It's not as if we do it every night, you know."

"It doesn't matter how often and it doesn't matter when. You took the health course last year and know that as well as I do. You've got to see your doctor *before* something happens."

"My mother might find out and she'd kill me," Lori said.

"So go to Planned Parenthood or go to my family doctor," Janet told her. There was the sound of a horn beeping outside the house.

"There he is," Lori said, looking around for her coat.

"Are you listening to me or am I talking to a brick wall?" Janet asked as Lori waved to Dave out the window.

"I hear you, I hear you—but suppose my mother finds out?"

"Then Dave could use something," Janet told her.

"Oh, cut out the doom and gloom," Lori aswered. "Nothing is going to happen, and even if I did get pregnant Dave wouldn't just take off and leave me. He wants to get married as soon as I finish school."

"It's not as simple as that," Janet pointed out. "You can't just leave everything up to Dave. You've got to think about your own life and your own future."

"Would you stop trying to cut down Dave?"

"I'm not cutting him down. I'm just trying to tell you the truth."

"Look," Lori shouted, "I don't need the truth or a lecture or anything because I can look after myself!" With that she rushed out the front door and slammed it shut behind her.

Ian was scared by the noise of the slamming door and started crying, so Janet rocked him in her arms to quiet him. She felt helpless in her anger at Lori, in even having tried to help. When the baby had stopped crying Janet could at last reach up and brush away her own tears from her cheek.

CHAPTER

Lori was in a rotten mood when she left Janet's house, and she took her feelings out on Dave. Dave got angry in return, wondering why Lori should be mad at him, and they had a fight. Lori ended up back at her house well before midnight.

But in a week the anger of that evening had passed. Dave's nightly phone calls had smoothed over the problems between them. Dave wrote a new song for Lori, a heavy rock number, and Lori said it was super. That night Lori had to sneak into the house again.

Still, Lori had been scared by some of

Janet's advice. In the two months that followed she and Dave forgot to be careful only once.

But once was enough.

Lori tried not to think about it. She had plenty of other problems to worry about. There was a term paper for Mr. O'Donnell, a low mark in English, and a project for her science class. But even while Lori worked on her school projects there was a fear in the back of her mind. It was no longer a fear of being found out but the awful fear that her luck had run out.

By April she was sure she was pregnant. Her period was late and she had begun to feel strange, a little ill, though not just in the mornings.

As Lori's fears began to grow she had more and more problems with Dave. She used the word "no" again and again with him, though she was afraid it was too late. They had fights more often. Lori would pick on Dave and he would get angry. But she said nothing to him of her fear of pregnancy, so Dave had no idea what lay behind the change in her.

Nor did Janet know what the problem

was. She and Lori were friends again, but they were not as close as they had been. Some of the trust between them had broken down that angry night at Janet's house.

So Lori carried her fears alone.

When her period was three weeks late Lori knew she couldn't wait any longer. In health class they had talked about a pregnancy test that you could buy at a drugstore. Lori thought that would be the easiest way, so she grabbed the bus to the Boots drugstore on Main Avenue. She felt guilty buying the kit even there, far from her house on the outskirts of Denver.

Still, Lori had to know.

The test had to be done in the morning, so Lori spent a sleepless night before she could use the kit. The test itself was simple. If a ring formed at the bottom of the test tube, it meant that she was pregnant. No ring meant that she was safe.

Lori's hands were shaking as she set up the test. When it was all mixed together she left the test tube in her room. Lori went downstairs to wait two

hours for the answer to her question, and they were the longest two hours in her life.

When the time had passed, Lori came quietly back into her bedroom. The sun was just rising and the light came beaming through her window. Lori hoped that might be a sign of good luck.

But it wasn't. A ring had formed at the bottom of the tube—Lori was pregnant.

Lori was too shocked to cry—she was too upset to do anything. For minutes she just stared at the test tube, wondering what would happen to her now.

At 8:30 her mother knocked on the door to ask if anything was wrong. Lori said that she was sick and couldn't go to school. Lori's mother didn't ask any more questions and left for work herself.

Lori knew there was a small chance that the drugstore test was wrong. She decided to phone Janet's doctor for a second test in order to know for sure.

"I'm sorry I had to keep you waiting so long," Dr. Lee said. "I asked the lab to rush this as fast as they could."

Lori sat in a wooden chair across from Dr. Lee. She didn't care about the hour she had spent waiting. She didn't care about anything but the answer to one question.

"Am I pregnant?" Lori asked.

"Yes," Dr. Lee told her. "The baby is due the third week of November."

Lori didn't know what to say. She felt like crying, but she had no tears.

"Have you and the father made any plans?" Dr. Lee went on.

"No," Lori said, her throat dry. "We talked about getting married once, but lately things haven't been too good."

Lori didn't have any plans—all she had were questions and fears, guilt, and a sense of being all alone. There were just too many things to think about to come up with plans.

Dr. Lee explained the choices that Lori and Dave had. Then she asked Lori to do some thinking—not just about herself right now, but about what she wanted for herself five years from now. Lori nodded and told Dr. Lee that she would think about things for a week. That gave her and Dave seven days to come up with a plan, to make a decision.

She called Dave from a pay telephone just outside the office.

"Dave, I have to see you right away," Lori told him.

"I can't right now, Lori," he said. "I'm in the middle of working out this new number."

"Right away, Dave," she cried into the phone.

"What's the matter?" he asked, surprised to hear tears in her voice.

"Dave," she said, her voice cracking, "I'm pregnant."

CHAPTER

"Are you sure?" is all Dave said as he opened the van door for Lori.

"I just came from the doctor's office," she told him. Her voice seemed cold, colder than she had wanted it to be.

"Where do you want to go?" he asked her.

"Anywhere—nowhere—just drive," Lori answered.

A silence fell between them for a few minutes while Dave drove the van through rush-hour traffic. The quiet seemed awkward to Lori, so she turned the radio on. Then the music bothered her, so she flipped it off.

"Make up your mind, huh?" Dave said to her.

"I'm trying," Lori mumbled. She was wondering how to start, how to begin the talk they'd both never wanted to have. It had been a mistake to tell him over the phone, but she hadn't been able to help herself. Now the fact of the baby stood between them and kept them apart.

"You must have guessed before now," Dave said after a while.

"About two weeks ago I started to worry, but I only just found out for sure," Lori told him.

"Why didn't you tell me before?" Dave asked, as if he were hurt by her hiding it from him.

"I thought I should wait until I was sure. Nobody else knows yet," Lori answered.

Lori could see how upset Dave was. She knew the way he wrinkled his forehead when things were bothering him. Now she could see the deep lines on his brow as he stared ahead at the street.

Lori wondered what he was thinking. It was Dave who had first talked about getting married, months ago. But then they had thought marriage would have to wait until the band was set up. Dave had said he wanted Lori to finish high school, as well. Did he still feel the same way?

Lori looked at the frown on Dave's face and wondered if she really wanted to marry him. It was not the first time she had asked herself that question. What good would be an eighteen-year-old husband who had never had a real job? Being pregnant made Lori look at Dave in a new way — not as a boyfriend, but as someone she might spend her life with.

"You don't have to stare at me," Dave said. "It's not just my fault, you know."

"Both of us were stupid," Lori admitted, near tears again. She tried to get back some control, but she couldn't. Lori started crying, only a little at first, but the sobbing grew as her fears and doubts flooded her mind. She had held back the tears since morning, but now there was no more holding back.

Dave heard her crying and pulled the van off the street into a parking lot. "Hey," he said, reaching over and touching her for the first time. "It'll be all right."

"I'm sorry, I'm sorry. I just can't help it," Lori sobbed. "I've been holding the whole thing in for so long, not talking to anybody, and now . . . ."

"It's O.K.," Dave said, drawing her wet face against his shoulder. "I love you and I'm not going to cut out on you or anything."

"Oh, I know that," Lori answered, though she hadn't been all that sure. "You have no idea what it's been like. Everything's been so awful, but I didn't want you to worry, because I wasn't sure,

because there was a chance."

"Yeah, but there's no chance any more, is there?"

"Well, the doctor said that it's still pretty early, so ... so I could stop it, you know."

"You mean an abortion," Dave said in a cold voice.

Lori nodded. She knew that abortion was one way out of the whole problem—maybe the fastest way. Not even her mother would have to know that she had gotten pregnant. Yet there was another part of Lori that couldn't accept that kind of choice. The child within her was small, but still it was a living being. Was it fair to end its life just because it would mess up her own life so much?

"No, I don't think you should have an abortion," Dave told her. "It's my baby, too, you know, and I think it has the right to be born."

"Maybe," Lori said, although she wasn't sure. "The doctor told me about a couple of other things we could do," she went on. "Of course, we could get married...." Lori waited a moment after she had said this, trying to catch the look on Dave's face. "Or I could have the baby without being married and wait until you think you're ready. Or we could give the baby up for adoption. The doctor says there are hundreds of couples just waiting to adopt a newborn."

"I don't like that much," Dave said, staring ahead at the rain falling outside. It was getting cold inside the van since he had shut off the motor.

"I guess we should both take some time to think about it. I told Dr. Lee that we would try to make a decision by next week."

"I don't really need time," Dave told her, his voice cracking. "I've already made my choice. I want to get married to you—right away, right now."

"Oh, Dave—I do love you!" Lori kissed him.

"I want to do the right thing," Dave went on, "and I want to give our baby a good life." Now Dave was crying. It was the first time Lori had ever seen him cry and she was surprised by the tears that were rolling down his cheeks. Dave had always seemed so strong and powerful singing with the band. Now, as she saw

his cheeks wet with tears, Lori knew that
he was strong enough to cry over the
future they faced.

Lori kissed the salty tears and held
Dave closer to her. He was so full of love
— but did that mean Lori should marry
him? Dave had made his decision quickly,
out of love, out of his sense of what was
right. Lori wondered how he would feel
tomorrow or in a year, or in ten years.
Was it a simple matter of being in love
and getting married and having a baby?

"What do you think, Lori?" Dave
whispered.

Lori thought about the question as she looked at him and stroked the side of his face. He seemed too young to become a father or a husband. "I don't know," Lori sighed. "I just don't know."

CHAPTER

Lori couldn't sleep that night or for days after that. There were too many choices, too many things to worry about for her to rest at night. The more Lori thought about being pregnant, the more confused she became.

By Sunday she knew she would have to talk to someone or go crazy. She thought of going to her mother, but it was too soon for that. She didn't want to face her mother until she and Dave had made up their minds about what to do.

So she went to Janet—not out of choice, but because there was no one else.

The worst part about telling her friend was that she had been right. If only Lori had listened to Janet's warnings, none of this would have happened.

"Have you been hiding out or something?" Janet asked as she answered the door.

"Well, I've been doing this and that," Lori said, stepping inside the house. "Your parents out?"

"Yeah, they've gone shopping, and Tammy took the baby down to get some milk at the store," Janet told her.

"I sort of wanted to talk to Tammy, too," Lori said.

"She'll be back from the store pretty soon. Something on your mind that you want to talk about?"

Lori didn't know where to begin. She couldn't just come out and say she was pregnant, but she couldn't keep the problem to herself, either.

"You and Dave having the usual problems?" Janet guessed, sensing that it might be much more than that.

"Yeah, only it's a lot worse than the usual problems," Lori began with a sigh. "It's ... Jan ... I'm pregnant."

73

"What?" Janet asked, her mouth dropping open. She had heard the words all right, but she didn't want to believe them.

"I'm almost six weeks pregnant now," Lori explained.

"Oh, Lori, I'm sorry," Janet said, as if she were ashamed to have asked.

Lori sank onto a kitchen chair and fought back the tears. She knew that if she started crying they'd both lose control.

"Dave wants to get married right away," Lori told her friend.

"Is that what you want?"

"I'm not sure—I can't seem to sort out all the choices and make a decision. That's why I came over here, Jan, so you and Tammy could help me make sense of everything."

Janet was upset to see Lori like this, too worried and confused to think. Before they could begin talking about it all, there was a noise at the front door.

"Sorry to break in," Tammy said, coming in with the baby.

She was about to leave the two girls alone when Lori called her back to the kitchen. "Tammy, we were waiting to talk to you," Lori told her.

"From the way you looked, I thought I'd walked in on some heavy stuff," Tammy said.

"You did," Lori said. "I just told Jan that I'm pregnant."

Tammy wasn't as shocked as Janet had been. She simply looked at Lori with concern and asked, "So now what?"

"That's what I want to talk about," Lori explained.

The three of them sat around the table while little Ian fell asleep in his mother's arms. There was so much that had to be said, about love, marriage, the baby, the choices. They talked of Dave, Lori's mom, the feelings between Dave and Lori—everything. But in the end they had to talk about the four things that Lori and Dave could do: get married, have the baby without getting married, give the baby up for adoption, or get an abortion. All this had to be clear before Lori and Dave could decide what to do.

"Something doesn't make sense," Tammy said. "Lori, you keep telling me that Dave loves you and wants to marry

you, and that's super. But what about you, Lori? Do you want to marry him?"

"I love him," Lori answered, repeating words she had said often enough.

"Are you sure?" Tammy asked her.

"Pretty sure. I mean, it isn't something that's happened to me a lot, you know."

"Yeah, I'm sorry—I didn't mean it like that," Tammy told her. "What I meant was, do you really think this is the guy you want to spend the rest of your life with? I think that's more important than whether or not you love him."

"I'm not sure," Lori said.

"I think getting married now would be an awful mistake," Janet broke in. The other two turned to look at her, surprised at the way she spoke her mind. "I'm sorry if that hurts you, Lori," she went on. "I've been keeping quiet for months now, and that hasn't done any good. So I'm going to say what I think. Dave is a super guy, but he's only eighteen and he's never even finished high school. Now it's one thing for him to say that he'll marry you, Lori, and be a good father, but it's another thing to do it."

"But he does love me," Lori said.

"O.K., but suppose you get married and Dave gets some crummy job and you take care of the baby," Janet went on. "He feels trapped, and you think he only married you because you were pregnant. His dream of being a big-time rock star is shot down, and you never get back to school. Does that sound like a love story?"

Lori shook her head.

"It doesn't have to be like that," Tammy pointed out. "Maybe Lori could get a job and Dave could take care of the baby for a while."

"Oh, sure," Janet said, shaking her head to show she didn't believe a word of it. "I think the whole idea of getting married because you're pregnant is no good. You should get married because you're in love and you're ready for it, not because you're forced into it."

"So what do you think we should do?" Lori asked.

"There's still time to get an abortion," Janet answered in a firm voice.

"Dave and I don't want to do that," Lori said.

"But you can ruin your life and the baby's life instead, eh? People always say that the baby has a right to life. Well, what about the baby's right to a *decent* life, a life with two people who are ready to be parents? Doesn't a baby have a right to be wanted?"

"Calm down, Jan," Tammy told her sister. "It's not as easy as you think. I've been in Lori's shoes and I know how she feels. That's *her* baby inside, and it's a hard thing to just end it all with an abortion."

"But you had your family to back you up," Janet said. "Lori's mother works and can't babysit the way mom does."

"What do you think, Lori?" Tammy asked. "Would your mother quit her job to look after the baby while you finished school?"

"She couldn't—there's not enough money now," Lori said.

"How would she feel about having a baby in the house if you dropped out of school to take care of it?"

"I guess my mother could put up with a baby all right," Lori answered. "But I don't like the idea of dropping out of school for a long time."

"Well, maybe it's time I stopped asking questions and gave my advice," Tammy said. "A lot of girls are doing what I'm doing—trying to bring up a baby by themselves. I admit I'm not the greatest parent in the world, but it's not easy. You have to be both parents rolled up in one. You have to keep going when the baby's sick, even when you're sick. You can't go out or do much of anything unless you can find a good sitter." Tammy waited for a moment, searching for the right words to say what she had to say.

"What I think is that Lori should give the baby up for adoption."

"I couldn't do that to my baby," Lori told her.

"So instead you'll try to bring the kid up yourself. You'll be tired, you won't have any money, and you'll be sick of it even before a year is out. That's doing the kid a favor?" Tammy asked.

Lori didn't answer—there wasn't any answer.

"Look," Tammy went on, "sometimes the nicest thing you can do for your baby is see that it gets a good home with two parents who'll really love it."

"I guess. If only all this had never happened," Lori sighed.

"Lori doesn't like any of the choices," Janet said. "They're all awful one way or another."

"You're right," Lori agreed. "All the choices are rotten, for *me*. But I'm not making a decision just for myself. I'm making one for the baby."

Lori still had to talk to her mother and to Dave, but she had made her decision—a decision that would hurt her.

CHAPTER

Seven months later.

When Janet got up to Lori's hospital room, her friend was packing her slippers.

"You almost set to go?" Janet asked, trying to be as cheerful as she could.

"Just about," Lori told her as she snapped the suitcase closed and looked around the ward for the last time. The three other beds were empty, so Lori and Janet were alone.

"Are you O.K.?" Janet asked. Lori's face was white, and she looked tense.

"Sure, Jan," Lori answered. She stood up and looked at herself in the mirror over the sink. She had been in the hospital five days since the baby was born, and for a lot of reasons she didn't want to leave.

"Your mother should be up here in a minute or two," Janet said.

Lori kept staring at herself in the mirror.

Janet came up beside her and put her arms around her. She gave Lori a hug because she looked so sad, so lost. Janet could guess at the hurt and doubts in her friend's heart.

"You're doing the right thing," Janet told her.

"I know, but that doesn't make it easy. Dave and I have been through all the reasons a hundred times, but it still hurts."

"Have you seen the baby yet this morning?" Janet asked.

"Not yet," Lori answered. "The nurse is going to bring him in for a feeding in a minute," she said, trying to smile.

Lori and Dave had decided many months ago to give the baby up for adoption. There had been days when Lori struggled against the decision, days when

she so wanted to keep the baby that the thought of losing him was more than she could bear. But Lori had stuck with the decision—not for herself, but for the baby.

The reasons were the right ones. At sixteen, Lori knew that she wasn't ready to get married, and after a while Dave had admitted he wasn't, either. Much as they dreamed of living together on their own—in the real world, it just wouldn't work.

Dave had no steady job and no skills to get one. Lori would be tied down with the baby. Neither family could give them help or money. And even in the world of dreams, Lori wondered if Dave was really the man she wanted as a husband. She never told Dave of these doubts, but they were there. And they counted.

The important thing, Lori knew, was to do what was best for the baby. Lori thought about the kind of home their baby deserved—loving parents who could take care of him properly. She knew that she could never give the baby that kind of home by herself.

Dr. Lee had told them that there were hundreds of couples wanting to adopt a baby. They could be sure he would be loved and cared for.

Dave had had a rough time dealing with the decision, too. He still felt he should marry her, that he should "do the right thing." It hurt him to admit that in the real world sometimes the right thing meant to let go. Dave had visited the hospital twice, but he couldn't stand to be with Lori and the baby on this, the last day. He had said his good-byes the day before.

Lori's mother had taken the news of

the pregnancy well and had given her daughter whatever backup she could. Lori was more surprised than anyone. She and her mother had been growing apart in the years before all this. Now they were together as they had been years ago, when Lori's father first left and all they had was each other.

"Are you ready, Lori?" her mother asked when she came to the door. "I've got you all checked out downstairs."

"I want to feed the baby one more time," Lori told her.

Lori's mother nodded, knowing how hard this must be for her.

The nurse brought the baby in a crib. He was crying the tiny cry of a hungry baby. Lori picked him up and he grew quiet. She held him gently in her arms and gave him a bottle.

Lori ran her fingers through the fine hair on the baby's head. He was such a beautiful baby! He had been born healthy and perfect, from his tiny toes to the little wrinkle between his eyes.

Lori's mother watched the baby as he nursed in her daughter's arms. She could see the love Lori felt for the baby in the

way she held him, in the gentle look she gave him. Behind Lori's eyes were tears, but in her eyes was only love.

"I brought something for the baby — sort of a special present," Janet said. She reached into her purse and pulled out a wrapped gift.

Lori put the bottle down and used her free hand to take off the wrapping paper. Inside were a tiny pair of booties for the baby.

"Oh, they're beautiful," Lori exclaimed.

"My mom showed me how to knit them," Janet told her.

Lori opened up the blanket that covered the baby. She touched the bottoms of both tiny feet with her finger and watched them curl up before she put on the booties.

"They're so cute," Lori's mother said.

Lori couldn't speak. She reached out for Janet's hand and squeezed it.

Then it was time.

The nurse was at the door to the room, waiting for the baby, and Lori herself was ready to go. The baby was asleep in her arms.

Lori kissed him gently on the forehead. The baby stirred in his sleep, opened his eyes and seemed to smile. Lori tried to whisper good-bye, but the word would not come out.

She kissed him once more as the nurse took him from her arms. Then, only then, did her tears begin to fall.

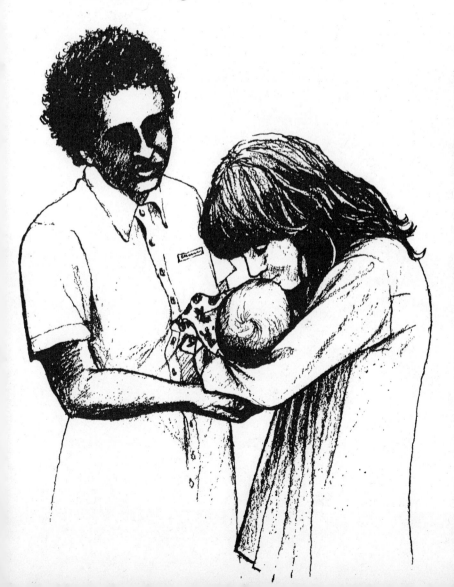

Other Encounters Titles

BURN OUT
Bob and Chewie have a plan to catch the firebugs on
Maple Street. The plan seems good at first. But when it
backfires, they get trapped in the basement of a burning
house.

DEAD ON
What is making the strange noises in the hall outside
Larry's room? It can't be a ghost. Larry doesn't believe in
ghosts. But someone — or something — keeps leading him
to the attic of the old house.

DIRT BIKE
Forty cycles roar out of the start chute. Randy races
toward the first turn on his yellow dirt bike. He looks
over at Bozo and grits his teeth. Only one of them can
come out the winner.

DOPE DEAL
Brian has to face a lot of problems. He gets busted by the
cops, has to move back home, and beats up his own
brother. But his biggest problem comes when he takes on
a whole motorcycle gang.

FAIR PLAY
When Andy Singh asks Carol to a party, she couldn't care
less whether his skin is black or white. But her old
boyfriend cares far too much. His jealousy and hate lead
to a night of danger on the icy streets of Windsor.

GANG WAR
Jack and the Punks think they're tough. But Charlie and
his friends don't like getting pushed around. The two
gangs fight it out in one last rumble.

HOT CARS
At first Robert doesn't know who is killing his dogs or wrecking his father's truck. When he gets trapped by a stolen-car gang, the answer almost kills him.

NO WAY
Pete just wants to show the others how brave he is. But his plan for the perfect rip-off falls apart. He ends up in trouble with the law. Now his old gang wants him to steal from the only people he really cares about.

RUNAWAY
Kathy wishes she were a goldfish. She has some good reasons — her father gets drunk and beats her, her best friend drives her crazy, and her boyfriend wants to get too friendly. Will she be better off if she runs away?

SNOW GHOST
Martin and Doug live through the plane crash, but the pilot is badly hurt. As they hike across the frozen bush for help, they're ready for anything. Except the snow ghost.

WILD ONE
Kate saves Wild One from Banner's whip and gets to train the horse herself. But that's only a start. Can she prove he can race before it's too late?